Read Along with Me Book & CD

Nursery Rhymes

AWARD PUBLICATIONS LIMITED

ISBN 978-1-84135-743-0

Copyright © 2010 Award Publications Limited
℗ 2010 Award Publications Limited

Illustrated by Suzy-Jane Tanner

Music composed by Tim King
Read by Sophie Aldred

First published 2010

Published by Award Publications Limited,
The Old Riding School, The Welbeck Estate,
Worksop, Nottinghamshire, S80 3LR

www.awardpublications.co.uk

09 1

Printed in China

The Queen of Hearts

The of

She made some

All on a summer's day;

The Knave of

He stole those

And took them clean away.

The  of

Called for the

And beat the Knave full sore.

The Knave of

Brought back the

And vowed he'd steal no more.

Humpty Dumpty

 sat on a wall,

 had a great fall.

All the King's ,

And all the King's men,

Couldn't put Humpty

together again.

Hey Diddle Diddle

Hey diddle diddle,

The  and the ,

The cow jumped over the .

The little laughed to see

such fun,

And the  ran away with

the spoon.

There Was an Old Woman
Who Lived in a Shoe

There was an  who

lived in a  .

She had so many ,

she didn't know what to do;

She gave them some

without any ;

Then spanked them all soundly

and put them to  .

The Crooked Man

There was a crooked ,

  and he walked a crooked mile.

He found a crooked sixpence

  beside a crooked 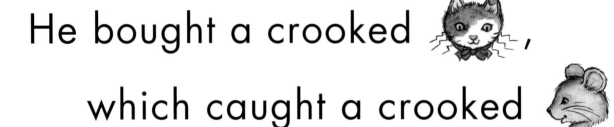.

He bought a crooked 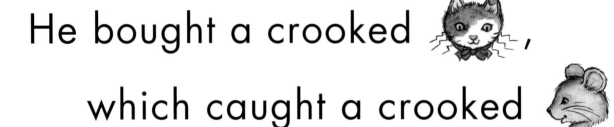,

  which caught a crooked,

And they all lived together in a

  little crooked house.

Jack and Jill

 and went up the hill,

To fetch a of water.

 fell down and broke

his crown,

And came tumbling after.

Then up  got and home

did trot,

As fast as he could caper;

He went to to mend

his head,

With vinegar and brown paper.

Old King Cole

Old  Cole was a merry

old soul,

And a merry old soul was he.

He called for his ,

And he called for his ,

And he called for his  three.

Every fiddler he had a fine  ,

And a very fine  had he.

Oh, there's none so rare, as

   can compare

With  Cole and his

   three.

Ride a Cock-Horse

Ride a  to Banbury Cross,

To see a fine lady upon a

white .

With on her fingers and

on her toes,

She shall have music wherever

she goes.

Little Miss Muffet

Little  sat on a ,

Eating her curds and whey.

There came a big ,

Who sat down beside her

And frightened away.

Hickory Dickory Dock

Hickory, dickory, dock,

The ran up the  .

The struck one,

The ran down,

Hickory, dickory, dock.

Baa, Baa, Black Sheep

Baa, baa, black ,

Have you any wool?

Yes sir, yes sir,

Three full;

One for the ,

And one for the dame,

And one for the little

Who lives down the lane.

Sing a Song of Sixpence

Sing a song of sixpence,

A pocket full of rye,

Four and twenty black

Baked in a  .

When the  was opened,

The began to sing;

Wasn't that a dainty dish

To set before the ?

The 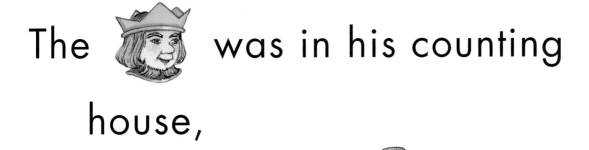 was in his counting

house,

Counting out his 🪙 ;

The 👑 was in the parlour,

Eating 🍞 and honey.

The 👩 was in the garden,

Hanging out the clothes,

When down came a blackbird,

And pecked off her ✂ .